IAN REDMOND

THE ELEPHANT BOOK

FOR THE ELEFRIENDS CAMPAIGN

illustrated with photographs

The Overlook Press

Woodstock · New York

DEDICATED TO

THE AFRICAN ELEPHANT

AND THOSE WHO ARE FIGHTING FOR ITS SURVIVAL

FIRST PUBLISHED IN 1991 BY

THE OVERLOOK PRESS

LEWIS HOLLOW ROAD

WOODSTOCK, NEW YORK 12498

PRINTED AND BOUND IN HONG KONG BY

THE SOUTH CHINA PRINTING COMPANY (1988) LTD.

LIBRARY OF CONGRESS CATALOGING-IN-PUBLICATION DATA

REDMOND, IAN.

THE ELEPHANT BOOK/IAN REDMOND

P.   CM.

ISBN 0-87951-432-9: $16.95

1. AFRICAN ELEPHANT. I. TITLE

QL737.P98R438 1991

599.6'1--DC20

91-6692

CIP

CONTENTS

My home in Nairobi National Park, Kenya, has become an orphanage for baby elephants. I have been looking after orphaned wild animals for forty years, but things have been getting worse for the elephants. Little calves are brought to me after they have witnessed their mother die in a hail of machine-gun bullets and the tusks hacked out of the still warm faces of their family. It is hardly surprising they are so hard to save – elephants are sensitive animals.

The orphans go through an intense period of grieving – from one to four months – when we must help them regain the will to live. They need intensive care – huge bottle feeds every three hours, day and night, and constant physical contact to replace their mother's tenderness. Through this work, I have come to know elephants intimately – more so, I think, than anyone else alive – not just in the wild, but as a foster mother to their orphaned young of all ages. My helpers and I have nursed them through their nightmares and slept with them in their straw beds. We have given them the will to live and to return to the wild, under the guidance of Eleanor, one of my first orphans, who now lives free in Tsavo National Park. But our work will not end until every consumer of ivory becomes an ELEFRIEND. Only then will the poaching stop and the babies be left in peace to grow up among elephants – where they belong.

Saving the world's elephants *must* be the responsibility of all thinking people. Every piece of ivory

is a haunting memory of a once-proud and majestic being, who has loved and been loved and was part of a close-knit and caring family similar to our own, but who has had to suffer and die in unspeakable agony to yield its tusks for trinkets and ornaments. That is a high price to pay for ivory and the world should want no part of it. We *can* replant forests, and even reclaim deserts in time, but no one, when the last elephant has gone, can make another.

Nairobi, 1990

"The death of an elephant, for me, is like the death of a human being. Elephants, too, feel pain and grief, are kind and compassionate, love their young and defend their territory against invaders. If we are indifferent to the slaughter and annihilation of this wise and wonderful animal, in order that we may buy ornaments or festoon ourselves with jewellery made from its teeth, we will have taken another irretraceable and shameful step towards our own physical and spiritual destruction."
Virginia McKenna, **ELEFRIENDS**

"Until we recognize what the real treasures of the world are, until we learn to share this earth with all its other inhabitants, we will find only temporary happiness. Is a miracle still possible? Could the enormity of the crime – the massacre over the past decade of almost a million elephants to satisfy human vanity and greed – sicken us enough to make us finally stop? Could it make us realize that we are pawning our own future for a handful of ivory beads? Could it make us realize that we must now draw up a universal charter of rights for all animals for their continued existence? If that happened then perhaps those million magnificent and noble elephants may not have died in vain."
Bill Travers, **ELEFRIENDS**

In 1989 the world finally woke up to what was happening to Africa's elephants. Their numbers had plummeted from an estimated 1.3 million to 609,000 in just ten years. The main cause was poaching for ivory. Up to 100,000 elephants were being slaughtered every year, their front teeth hacked out, their bodies left to rot, their tiny calves left to die of starvation. If nothing was done, the downwards curve on

the population graph would soon hit zero. The unthinkable was suddenly being talked about – extinction. But this was not news to everyone; the signs had been there for a long time.

It was not elephants but gorillas that first drew me to Africa. In 1976, I joined the late Dr Dian Fossey in Rwanda, to assist with her research and conservation work among the mountain gorillas. The gorillas share the misty, tangled slopes of the Virunga Volcanoes with forest elephants, and Dian used to regale me with tales of elephants coming down to drink from Camp Stream, and then scratching their bottoms on the corner of her corrugated iron cabin, making it sway alarmingly. Sadly, I was too late to share in those experiences. The last of the resident elephants around the Karisoke Research Centre was shot by ivory poachers in 1975, despite being in the middle of a National Park.

It was not until 1980 that I became really hooked on elephants. In Kenya, I joined an Operation Drake project to "build a tourist path up to Kitum Cave in the Mount Elgon National Park, and to monitor the cave for elephants." After witnessing a herd of elephants feeling their way by moonlight into the black maw of Kitum Cave, I knew that I had to find out more about this little-known phenomenon.

Happily, ivory poaching was not a problem here, and for several years I did not fear unduly for these elephants because the mining activity wears down the tusks to mere stumps. It seemed to me unlikely that ivory poachers would risk the dangers of hunting in a cold, wet montane rainforest patrolled by park guards, for such poor quality ivory.

I was wrong. Such is the demand for ivory around the world, that even the scratched and pitted tusks of the Elgon elephants were considered profitable. In 1987, I returned to Elgon to investigate reports of poaching. As I approached Kitum Cave the stench of death reached me. There on the forest floor lay the mutilated carcass of a 12-year old bull. A seething mass of maggots spilled out from the thick, brown skin; the skull was cut in a single plane – the work of a chain saw. Nearby were the decomposing remains of a three-year-old calf from the same attack – they had been ambushed in the mouth of the cave. Standing there, I felt an enormous surge of anger and sadness.

Ivory is not a rock or a wood. It is a dead elephant's tooth. And as long as there is a demand for the ivory earrings, bangles, statuettes and knick-knacks that adorn the wealthy and their homes, someone is going to go out and kill elephants to get a share of that wealth. It is impossible to protect every wild elephant all of the time, but the need for such intensive protection would evaporate if ivory lost its value. And ivory *would* lose its value if none of us would buy it.

"We've had Save the Whale. Now it is time to Save the Elephant."
Dr Iain Douglas-Hamilton, Nairobi

Already attitudes are changing; in May 1989 Tanzania was the first nation to propose a ban on the ivory trade, and the ELEFRIENDS campaign was launched in London; in July, Kenya's President

"Blackened tusks formed the splintered and charred backdrop to a crescent moon of, as yet, unmarked ivory. To some, it may have seemed like a glimpse into an elephant hell, but for me it was not the fire of destruction but one of hope."
Will Travers, Nairobi

Daniel arap Moi bravely burned 12 tonnes of confiscated ivory – proving to the world that he was serious about ending the ivory trade; and in October, the nations in CITES (the Convention on International Trade in Endangered Species of Wild Fauna and Flora) voted for a ban on commercial trade in ivory. This ban will be reviewed in 1992 which gives the ELEFRIENDS just one year to change the world's attitude to ivory. With your help, we will succeed. Please take a personal pledge never to buy or use ivory in any form. And please complain if ever you see ivory on sale.

By these simple means, we can all help to Save the Elephant.　　Ian Redmond, Bristol 1990.

Amagnificent bull elephant strides slowly across the savannah. Suddenly he stops to listen, ears spread like sails as if to assist his passage over the sea of grass. What he hears are the deep rumblings of other bulls, or perhaps a female telling him she is ready to mate. Whatever the message, it is carried across the bush by low-frequency sounds, well below the level of human hearing. It wasn't until 1986 that scientists learned that there is more to elephant-talk than meets the human ear.

This discovery served to remind us that there is still much to learn about elephants. They play a central role in the ecology of Africa and many other species of animals and plants could not survive without them.

"The thought of Africa without elephants is appalling." Sir David Attenborough

An elephant's face is unlike any other in the animal kingdom. It has only two front teeth, and these stick out to form the tusks, which continue to grow throughout the elephant's life – except for those of the female Asian elephant (above left) which remain small and largely hidden. An elephant uses its tusks both as weapons – in threat displays and actual combat – and as tools: for digging up roots or mineral-rich earth, for stripping bark and for lifting things with the aid of its trunk.

The elephant's nose and upper lip have become fused and extended to form a novel kind of fifth limb. The Swahili word for trunk is "mkono", meaning hand, because the trunk is used to hold and manipulate things. As a hand, however, it is unique, being equipped with an acute sense of smell as well as touch, and no bones. The lack of bones means that a trunk can bend, fold or curve in any direction; it is controlled by about 100,000 muscles that criss-cross and work against each other all the way to the tip. An African elephant's nostrils emerge at the tip of the trunk between two flexible "fingers". So precise is the movement of these trunk-fingers, that an elephant can delicately wipe a piece of grit from its eye, or pick up a single seed from the ground.

The trunk also serves as an early warning system, ever alert to a whiff of danger. If an elephant senses the presence of humans or other predators, it holds its trunk aloft like a nasal periscope to sample the breeze.

An elephant does not perceive the world in the same way that we do. Sight, which for humans is the sense that tells us most about our surroundings, comes a poor third for elephants, behind the senses of smell and hearing.

"I welcome this opportunity to support the international efforts to protect these magnificent beings."
Dr Jane Goodall

In proportion to its body size, an elephant's eye seems rather small, being about the same size as a human eye. The iris is normally brown, but it is often hard to see because it is shaded by a very impressive set of eyelashes that sweep out from the upper eyelid. With its eyes placed on either side of its head, an elephant – like a horse – has an almost all-round field of vision, with only a small area directly in front where the sight of both eyes overlaps. But the retina in an elephant's eye has far fewer light-sensitive cells than a human eye, and so its

sight is rather poor – particularly in bright light and at distances of more than about thirty paces.

Elephants can hear a remarkably wide range of sounds, from the tiny high-pitched squeaks and chirrups which they apparently make with their trunks, to the powerful infrasonic rumbles with which they communicate over great areas of bush.

The size of the outer ear, however, has less to do with hearing than with temperature control. When an elephant flaps its ears – or stands into the wind with ears held out to catch the breeze – the moving air takes away excess body-heat. The ears are equipped with a network of large blood-vessels which act like radiator pipes. These blood-vessels give out heat and, as a result, the blood *leaving* the ear vessels is several degrees cooler than when it entered them. This may be why the Asian elephant – which dwells more in shady forests – has smaller ears than the African species, and why the African forest elephant, in its turn, has much smaller ears than the African bush elephant.

Between the eye and the ear of an elephant lies the temporal gland – visible as a small, slit-like opening from which a dark fluid often trickles. Behind the slit is a large gland – weighing up to one and a half kilos in a bull elephant – whose function is not fully understood. In Asian

elephants, temporal fluid only flows from a male in "musth" (see page 28), but it often flows in both sexes of the African elephant for no obvious reason. When an African bull *is* in musth, however, his temporal glands swell and secrete a darker, oily fluid which he rubs on vegetation as a scented signpost to advertise the fact that he is in musth.

"The shape of an African elephant's ear is the shape of Africa...As if Nature had kept an ear to the ground when listening to the elephant's territorial requests."
Heathcote Williams

The longest hairs on an elephant's body are those on the top and bottom of its tail. Each hair is like a thick, glossy black wire, up to three-quarters of a metre in length.

Elephant skin feels rough to a human hand, but this does not mean that it is insensitive. Beneath the tough, horny outer layer there are touch receptors that can pin-point an irritating insect – to be brushed off by a precise swing of the trunk or, at the rear, by a flick of the tail.

The folds and wrinkles in the skin serve to trap moisture which slowly evaporates to cool the elephant.

The texture of an elephant's skin varies, from the thick, calloused folds of the forehead to the soft, thin pliable skin behind the ears and under the belly.

The soles of the feet are thickened into ridges, like the cleats on the sole of a climbing boot. This gives elephants a good grip when negotiating the steep cliffs and escarpments that they climb with such surprising ease.

Elephants walk on the tips of their fingers and toes.

"The elephant intrigues me so much, its strength and dignity, its silent movement and sudden trumpeting fury, the humour of its young, the threatening beauty of its tusks, the delicate touch of its trunk and the intelligent look in its wise old eye – all these enthralled me."
the late George Adamson

Inside each foot, the digits rise from the nails on the outside to meet the wrist or heel bones; these rest on a fibrous pad, inside the foot, which acts as a kind of shock absorber.

There are usually five nails on the forefoot, which is round, and four on the more oval-shaped hindfoot. When an elephant "kneels" on its front legs, it is actually resting on its wrists; the true knees (with knee-caps) are found only on the hind legs, as in humans. When an elephant stands at rest, the bones in each limb stack to form the sturdy columns which bear up to six tonnes of elephant!

The most familiar habitat for African elephants is the savannah, or "bush" – a vast expanse of rolling grassland, dotted with flat-topped acacia trees and divided by winding strips of riverine forest. It is familiar because, of all the elephant habitats, it is the most accessible.

During the rainy seasons, when the grass is green and growing, elephants can be found all across the savannah – tearing up great tussocks with their trunks, beating away the soil and shearing off unwanted roots with a grind of their molars. Later, when the rains end and the grass yellows and dries, they spend more time in the patches of woodland along river banks. Here the ground is moist and the trees, with their deeper roots, remain green for longer and provide nourishing browse.

The forest elephants of Africa are usually the forgotten elephants. Little is known of their behaviour and they are seldom filmed or photographed. And yet a recent estimate put the number of elephants within the rainforests at 214,000 – about thirty-five per cent of the continental total.

The true forest elephant is a sub-species which has smaller, more rounded ears, downward-pointing brownish-yellow tusks and is smaller than the more familiar bush elephant. These differences seem to be adaptations to a forest life where, for example, large sweeping tusks would be a disadvantage when pushing through undergrowth.

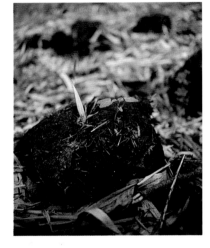

The ecological importance of elephants cannot be overstated. If the rainforest is seen as a life-generating machine, then the elephant is one of its main cogs. One-third of the many tree species in West African forests rely on elephants to eat their fruit and thereby disperse their seeds in the dung. Some tree seeds will not germinate *unless* they have been passed through an elephant's gut and been deposited in the rich package of manure that is an elephant's dung-ball.

"A fully grown elephant has little to fear from other animals. He is their essential friend, he makes their roads, he digs their water in dry sand river beds and he scatters seeds to regenerate the land. Who are we to say he must die?"
Bill Travers

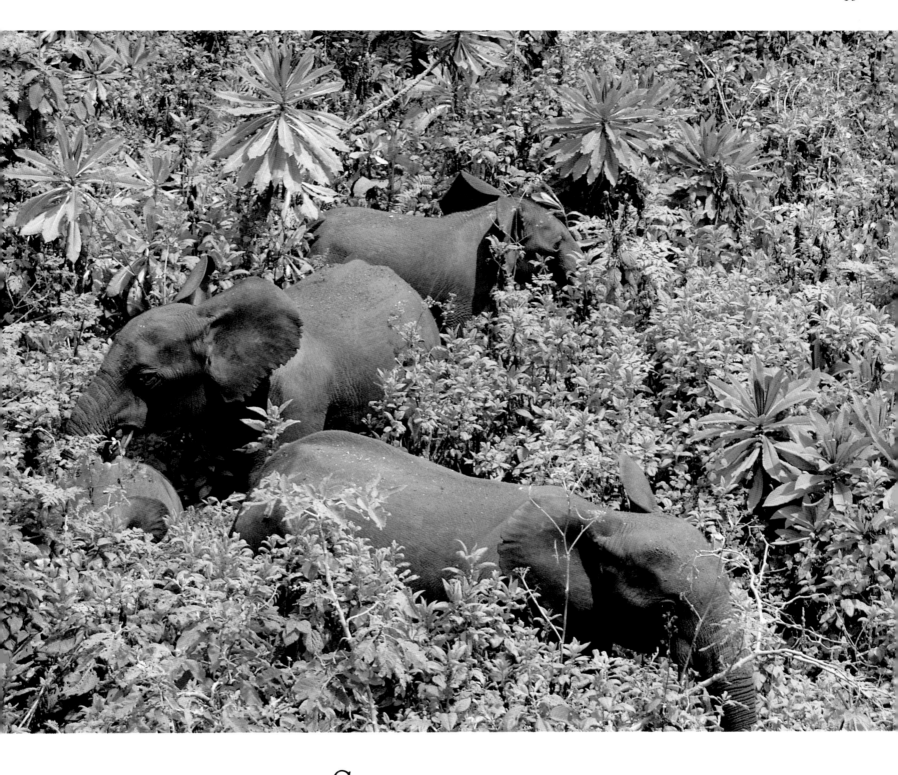

Sometimes there may not be enough light for the seedling to grow. But when a passing elephant pushes over a nearby tree, breaking the forest canopy and creating a glade, life-giving sunlight can reach the ground and the seedlings will start to grow. Ground-level herbaceous plants grow rampantly in such sunny patches, providing food for forest antelopes and enriching the habitat.

"For most people, the elephant is a fact; a huge familiar silhouette that will always

exist. Not true. It is already late in the day. We must, each of us, keep this social and

magnificent animal on this planet."

Betty White

Among the creeping, windblown sand dunes or the parched, thorny scrub of the Huab Desert in Namibia, the last thing one might expect to see is a water-loving animal such as an elephant. But like people, elephants have the ability and intelligence to modify their habitat; this enables them to live in the arid conditions of the Huab and other African deserts. Despite the dessicated vegetation and low annual rainfall, elephants survive in these areas because they can dig down in dry riverbeds to reach water.

The water may be as much as two metres below the surface but, with tusks and trunk, an elephant can excavate a deep seep-hole, and then wait patiently for it to fill before lifting each trunkful of the precious liquid to its mouth.

Knowledge of the best places to dig for water is handed down from generation to generation. As such it is a form of "elephant culture", and each separate population of desert elephants has its own unique traditions.

In the same way that human tribes benefit from the knowledge of former generations, elephants, too, increase their chances of survival. If the last desert elephant were to die, this cultural knowledge would also disappear, and it is unlikely that any future elephants, reintroduced from elsewhere, could succeed without it.

Elephants are seldom found very far from water. Every day they make their way down to a river, lake or forest pool to drink. The arrival is usually a leisurely affair, as smaller groups within the herd enter the water in their own time.

After the elephants have quenched their thirst, there is then time to bathe and relax. Their dusty, quilted skins are dunked and showered, and liberally plastered with mud. And while there is a serious side to this activity – keeping their skin cool and moist under the hot African sun – it also offers a great opportunity for elephantine fun. Calves wriggle, wrestle and roll in the mud, emerging like chocolate-coated elephants to challenge their playmates. Even adults seem to drop all dignity at times and act plain silly, throwing trunk-fulls of water around like overgrown schoolboys.

Elephants, like all other animals, need salt. If their food does not contain enough, they will search until they find a salt-lick – an outcrop of mineral-rich strata. But, unlike the other salt-hungry animals, elephants cannot actually lick the salt. Their tongues are simply not long enough to reach around their trunks and tusks. Instead, they dig it up. Using their tusks like a spade to loosen the earth, elephants pick up the clods with the delicate tip of their trunks and put them into their mouths. Even rocks, if they are salty, are ground up by the massive molars and swallowed.

"Hindoo mythology teaches that the earth is supported by eight elephants ... In the Ramayana, is a very curious account of the journey of a party of men who penetrated to the interior of the earth, and had an audience with the famous elephants."

Charles F Holder, The Ivory King

Elephant salt-digging behaviour has undercut cliffs in some parts of Africa and Asia, but in only one place has it resulted in large caves – on Mount Elgon in Kenya.

In the dark recesses of these huge caverns, elephants feel their way to traditional mining bays deep underground. There, working only by touch, they use their tusks as living ivory chisels to prise off lumps of sodium-rich volcanic ash to eat. From their earliest days, baby elephants accompany their mothers right into the caves. The cows, however, keep a careful trunk on their offspring to prevent them wandering off and falling down a crevasse or rock face in the pitch-dark interior.

The leadership of a family herd of elephants always rests with a venerable old female, known as the matriarch. The herd she leads normally consists of her daughters and grand-daughters, with perhaps one or two sisters and their offspring as well. These interrelated females co-operate in raising their young, even to the extent that one elephant mother will some-times suckle another's baby.

When danger threatens, all the family members turn to the matriarch for guidance. Her behaviour, based on decades of experience, will tell them whether to fight or flee. She may lead them to form a defensive circle, with the calves safely inside and the adults facing outwards, ears spread and heads held high to increase their apparent size and intimidate the foe.

If members of a family become separated, they

appear anxious and try to keep in touch with long-distance calls, called "contact rumbles". When they come together again, they go through a special greeting ceremony which involves rumbling, trumpeting, urinating and defecating in a tight ring, with heads and tails held high. This greeting is reserved for closely-related individuals, and so when two different families meet and greet with excitement, it usually means that some of the elder cows are relatives who grew up together and have kept in touch over the years. Few animals other than humans live in such a complex social network, where the relationships span decades rather than years or months.

"After eighteen years of watching

elephants I still feel a tremendous thrill

at witnessing a greeting ceremony...

I have no doubt even in my most

scientifically rigorous moments that the

elephants are experiencing joy when

they find each other again...

it is elephantine joy and it plays a very

important part in their whole

social system."

Cynthia Moss, Elephant Memories

The matriarch will not tolerate adult bulls to live within the family unit on a regular, day-to-day, basis. When one of the females comes into oestrus, however, and is ready to mate, bulls can often be seen hanging around the outskirts of the herd, displaying their strength and vying for her attentions.

Once they reach maturity, bull elephants spend most of their time alone or with other bulls. They may form loose associations with other males, but these bachelor herds are not based on long-term social bonds like those of females. One or two young bulls are sometimes seen with a very old tusker – which led the white hunters to dub them "askaris" – meaning soldiers or guards. Their presence would certainly help to thwart an attack by a trophy-hunter or ivory-poacher (to the elephant the difference is irrelevant), but it may be the young bulls who benefit most from the relationship. The older, more experienced bull passes on his knowledge of "elephant politics" and of how to survive adverse conditions such as drought.

Male elephants indulge in frequent trials of strength called sparring. These mock fights serve to establish a hierarchy based mainly on size and strength. Because elephants have such good memories, they not only recognize the other males they come across but also know their relative social standing without having to fight to re-establish it whenever they meet.

The one thing which regularly disrupts this organized male society is the onset of musth. African bulls only begin to show musth in their mid-twenties, and only for a short time each year. It is a period of risk-taking when they rush around with heads held high, challenging other bulls, secreting from their temporal glands, giving special low-frequency musth rumbles and leaving behind them a trail of strong-smelling urine wherever they wander.

"In their response to danger, every bull usually looks after himself, which makes it all the more remarkable that bulls do sometimes help others which have been wounded..."
Dr Iain Douglas-Hamilton,
Among The Elephants

Other, more dominant, males may even back down from a younger male in musth. As they get older, the musth period becomes longer and more regular, but it is always a drain on the bull, because so little time is spent feeding. However, for most of the year, the bulls feed quietly and spar good-naturedly to build up their strength for this all-out period of fighting and mating. A fight between two musth bulls is one of the most impressive sights in nature, and may sometimes be a fight to the death.

When a bull elephant passes through a family herd, he is alert to the subtle scents of the females. A female elephant is in oestrus – able to conceive – for only a few days each year and so the bull reaches out his trunk and then curls it to a special organ in the roof of his mouth to test whether any of the cows are receptive. If one is, she might move off with head held high, inviting him to chase her and giving low sexy rumbles. She will run fast and not stop for young bulls, but for a big dominant bull she will slow down after a time, allowing him to catch up and lay a gentle trunk across her back.

> *"The manoeuvering of the males around an oestrus female is like a well-choreographed dance in slow motion; each step the female takes is mirrored by the musth male..."*
>
> **Dr Joyce Poole, Animal Kingdom**

Female elephants do seem to choose who they mate with, and usually show a clear preference for a large musth bull in his prime – between thirty-five and forty-five years of age. He will try to stay with her as a consort and guard her against other males until the end of her oestrus when conception occurs.

To avoid too great a crush on his partner, the bull will lightly rest his tusks and forefeet along her back when mating, but he will take most of his weight on his own hind legs. Afterwards, the female gives a series of low calls which prompt her family to join her in what is termed a "mating pandemonium". All the females "rumble, scream, trumpet, urinate, defecate and secrete from their temporal glands in a contagious frenzy of activity" which presumably advertises the presence of an oestrus female to any other males within earshot. As each bull arrives, he inhales the exciting scent of oestrus, while she extends a welcoming trunk to investigate his state of musth. To mate, however, he has to separate her from her consort – a system which ensures that it is the biggest and most powerful bull who finally fathers her next calf.

The birth of a baby elephant is an event of great interest to all in the family herd. The new mother is usually attended during labour by another cow – the "midwife" – as she moves restlessly and prepares herself for the birth.

With a gentle nudge from its mother, a newborn calf can usually wobble to its feet within half an hour of birth, but is totally dependent on her for food, protection and instruction. A baby elephant's sense of security comes from within a palisade of huge pillar-like legs; reassurance is the gentle caress of a trunk. Until one year of age, a calf can take shelter beneath the rumbling girth of its mother's chest. There too, between the cow's front legs, he will find sustenance.

To feed, a baby elephant reaches upward, curls its funny little trunk onto its forehead and drinks sucking with the mouth, not the trunk. A female elephant has breasts similar in size and shape to those of a woman, except that the nipples are angled sideways, making it easier for the baby to reach as he stands at her side. The mother, by simply moving one leg forward, can continue to reach for her own food while her calf feeds.

"The elephant is a symbol of much that we aspire to ourselves – strength, dignity, wisdom, humour and close family ties. We owe it to our children and to the elephant himself, to reverse in the 1990's the tide of destruction that swept through Africa during the 1980's."
Philip Cayford, Wildlife film - maker

The baby is born after a twenty-two month gestation period – the longest in the animal kingdom. Births can occur at any time of the year, but there is a peak in numbers during the rainy season, when there is a rich supply of fresh green vegetation for nursing mothers. This peak occurs because the biggest breeding bulls time the onset of their musth to coincide with the rains, thereby giving their calves the best chance of survival when they are born nearly two years later.

Although a single calf is the norm, twins are occasionally born, and both calves may survive if food is plentiful.

Young elephants are filled with an insatiable curiosity about their surroundings. The main organ of exploration is, of course, the trunk. But for the first few months, baby elephants have no idea how to control that rubbery appendage. With their oversized ears and undersized trunks, they look and behave more like cartoon characters than real elephants. Less than impressive threat displays are directed at all and sundry – even butterflies or birds – but if anything threatens *it*, the calf is quick to scuttle back to its mother. The calves have a lot to learn. Like humans and apes, elephants have a long childhood during which they absorb the knowledge of their elders. The strongest bond in elephant society is that between a mother and her calf. A male calf is more

demanding and the mother usually gives in to his tantrums. She suckles him more often and he grows faster than his sisters. But both sexes soon learn that they must keep up when, for example, it is time to leave the waterhole. If they lag behind, there is always an aunt or a sister to lend a friendly helping trunk.

While their mothers are feeding, much of the calves' time is spent in rough-house play with their friends – favourite games being "Push of War" and "Climbing on Top of Your Playmate".

Once the matriarchs are gone, who will teach the orphans the greeting rumble and who will be left for them to greet?"
Dr Joyce Poole

The differences between the behaviour of male and female calves become more marked as young elephants approach adolescence. Sexual maturity in both sexes comes between eight and thirteen years of age, but social maturity is different. A cow is likely to give birth to her first calf during her early teens, with the support and reassurance of her mother and aunts. A bull, on the other hand, is unlikely to father any offspring until he is in his thirties and is able to compete with older, more dominant males.

For the males, the boisterous games of calfhood gradually develop into the more serious sparring of young bulls. The forests ring with the clack of ivory on ivory as they fence with their tusks, and trials of strength are settled by head-on shoving matches and bouts of trunk-wrestling. Once the rapidly growing bulls begin to take an interest in oestrus females, they are ejected from the family herd by the matriarch, and will spend a decade building up their strength and experience before the first signs of musth appear, and the prospect of success in courtship.

"Hundreds of elephants are killed so that people can wear ivory bracelets. This is wrong — something must be done about this. I believe that the elephant is our dinosaur — the elephant is in a class by itself. We must protect our dinosaurs. The elephant is a treasure to the world and the world must protect this treasure."
James Stewart, Actor

As female calves grow up, they grow out of play-fighting games and begin to take on some of the duties of looking after the younger babies in the herd. Calves are usually weaned during their third year, and the interval between births is about five years. This means that, as the second calf begins to explore, an older sister (or cousin if the first baby was male) is on hand to help. This nursemaid role of the young females is of great importance to both animals. The nursemaid gains by learning some of the skills of motherhood, and the smaller calf gains by increased protection and a greater sense of security. If a mother dies after her young calf has been weaned, it is far more likely to survive if a nursemaid is on hand to look after it.

Elephants have huge appetites. They spend about three-quarters of each day and night gathering trunkful after trunkful of food – up to 225 kilos per day for an adult bull. They are selective feeders, but because the trunk can both smell and touch things at the same time, it can select, pick and, if need be, prepare each morsel without its owner necessarily looking at the food before it is put into its mouth. The range of food types available to an elephant is unparalleled; by standing up on its hind legs, an elephant with outstretched trunk can reach leaves higher than a giraffe; by shaking the whole tree, an elephant can bring ripe fruit down to the ground; by tusking the earth, roots and tubers can be dug up; and by wading out into swamps, lush grasses can be gathered.

"To be within a few feet of a group of sleeping elephants at night is a profoundly moving and peaceful experience... Few other animals would dare to abandon themselves to such luxuriously profound slumber in the dangerous African bush."
Dr S Keith Eltringham, Elephants

There are three main feeding bouts each day – during the morning, afternoon and in the middle of the night

– with time in between for digestion and other activities. During the heat of the day, elephants will seek shade and relax, but the main rest period is in the early hours of the morning before dawn. Elephants fall into a deep sleep for between one and four hours each night, often snoring contentedly. Very

large elephants may sleep standing up, but most lie down on one side.

Elephants have a thirst that is almost equal to their appetite for food, but they usually visit water only once or twice each day. The trunk is used to lift water to the mouth, but not like a drinking straw. Each draught is drawn up into the trunk, then the end of the trunk is shut tight and curled into the mouth. The elephant then tilts its head back, opens its trunk and lets the water gush down its throat. Skin care is another daily activity. This involves a combination of bathing (using the trunk as a built-in shower attachment), dusting, plastering with mud and scratching. Bathing is both a means of keeping cool and of keeping the skin soft and supple. A bath is often

followed by a mud-pack or a thorough dusting, which prolongs the cooling period and acts as a sun-screen to protect the skin from sunburn.

Layers of dried mud and dead skin are later rubbed off against a tree-trunk or a conveniently shaped boulder. Elephants are among that elite group of animals that can make and use tools, and if an itch is in an awkward place, a stick may be grasped in the trunk and used to scratch it.

One of the most moving and mysterious facets of elephant behaviour is the way they treat their dead. Elephants show a strong interest in the remains of deceased elephants – particularly of late relatives – whether they have died recently or some years before. They slowly feel over the body or skeleton with the trunk tip, as if recalling the individual they once knew, and will often pick up and scatter old bones and tusks.

Kyle Owens, who was working in Burkina Faso in 1986, witnessed a remarkable scene. While watching a herd of eight elephants with a tiny baby, he saw that the baby was ill. Throughout the morning the mother tried everything to raise the calf to its feet: "She dropped to her knees and lifted the baby with her trunk. She gently rocked him to an upright position with her forefoot. Each time the baby fell back onto his side with a scream, and each time the mother screamed too…the frustration, hope and suffering brought tears to my eyes.

At dusk I returned. The baby had died. His tiny body was barely visible as the other elephants had covered him with dirt, grass and leaves. The mother positioned herself over her child and began to rock. Occasionally another elephant would stroke her back affectionately, or intertwine trunks, but she continued to rock as darkness fell".

Another zoologist, Dr J "Hezy" Shoshani, was visiting Amboseli in Kenya with friends: "We came across the carcass of an elephant, and a female with her calf was standing nearby. They moved into the bushes and we stopped to take a look at the decomposing body. I began to cut a small section of skin to show my students, when suddenly the female appeared from the bushes, spread her ears and charged from about fifteen paces!" The resulting confusion was comical in retrospect, but the point of the story is more profound. The female resumed her position standing over the body; she had made them realize that it wasn't just a dead elephant lying there. It was a living elephant's dead relative or friend.

"It was a ceremony, a funeral of sorts. A complex and

intricate ritual conducted by elephants in honour of their

fallen brother. The experience will be with me forever

as a constant reminder of the magnificence, intelligence

and compassion of elephants."

Kyle Owens

The crisis now facing both species of elephant represents the final stages of a process which began thousands of years ago. It is no exaggeration to say that elephants were once the dominant species throughout most of Africa and southern Asia. Elephants lived almost everywhere, out-numbering by far the scattered tribes of *Homo sapiens*. During the period of recorded history, however, elephant numbers and range have been steadily reduced as a direct result of human activity.

Much of Africa and Asia is now a cultivated landscape, criss-crossed by roads and fences and dotted with modern cities. There are still islands of elephants in this sea of humanity, but these are rapidly shrinking in the face of an expanding human population.

Every rural family wants its little patch of land to cultivate, but it is often said that "one cannot share an acre with an elephant". In terms of temperature, rainfall and soil fertility, elephants have the same sort of requirements as humans. As a result, elephants are steadily being evicted from their former range, which they later visit – an activity that people call "crop-raiding". This loss of habitat presents the greatest long-term threat to elephant survival, but the network of parks and reserves would be enough to save the species IF the poaching could be stopped.

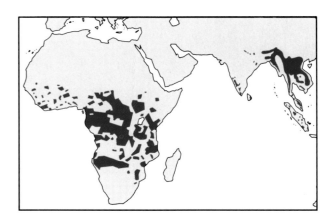

The present, scattered distribution of elephant populations in Africa and Asia.

"Why don't they just let the elephants die of old age, then their tusks will be bigger and they can just pick them up off the ground without shooting?"
Matthew Gamble, 8-year-old schoolboy

The ivory trade is illogical. Complex computer models of trade data have confirmed what is obvious to a child – the most profitable way of managing a population of elephants is to let them die of old age. This is because to the carvers of luxury ornaments in places such as Hong Kong and Japan, ivory in the form of large tusks is worth more per kilo than the same weight made up of small tusks; also, old elephants have already produced the next generation. A herd of elephants is the nearest thing in real life to the fairytale goose that laid the golden egg. But the poachers are in the process of killing the golden goose itself.

Driven by an apparently insatiable demand for ivory and the desire for profits *now*, the poachers – and ninety-four per cent of ivory stems from poaching even if rangers recover the tusks and these are then sold legally – have been killing elephants of all ages and both sexes. This is reflected in the trade statistics. The ivory trade grew steadily between 1950 – when 204 tonnes of tusks were sold – and 1983 when the figure was 1,000 tonnes. The annual total then began to fall: 600 tonnes in 1986; 300 tonnes in 1987. But this did not mean that fewer elephants were being killed. In 1979, one

"It is a pity that an intelligent creature like the elephant should be shot in order that creatures not much more intelligent may play billiards with balls made from their teeth."
Captain Richard Meinertzhagen, Kenyan Diary, 1903

tonne of ivory represented fifty-four dead elephants – mainly bulls with large tusks (average weight: 9.3 kg). By 1987, most mature bulls had been shot, and so cows and calves were being killed for their smaller tusks (average weight: 4.7 kg). Thus one tonne of ivory in 1987 came from 113 dead elephants by

tusk weight, but many of them were adult females, so a further fifty-five calves (with no ivory) were orphaned and left to die of starvation.

One thing is clear from these statistics. If we do not voluntarily end the ivory trade now, the trade will end itself before too long, by wiping out the source of its raw material.

In Asia, the elephant is venerated. Domestic elephants still play a vital role in carrying timber and tourists through the forests, and as the bearer of royalty or religious relics in processions. But only 35,000 Asian elephants survive, of which one third are domestic. And unlike any other domestic animal, each new generation is captured from the wild and trained. As numbers dwindle, such captures now threaten the survival of some wild herds.

Is it possible for humans and elephants to coexist peacefully? In the very heart of Africa, on the shores of a lake, lies a fishing village called Vitshumbi. It is located in the Virunga National Park, Zaire, but the wealth of the village stems from fishing, not from poaching. The villagers are so tolerant that when elephants wandered down the main street, their passage prompted little reaction from the residents.

Sadly, those elephants were badly hit by the ivory gangs, but the principle remains. Where there is no conflict, humans *can* live alongside elephants.

Thanks to the rise in eco-tourism, elephants are worth more alive than dead. Land set aside for elephants can earn more than almost any other form of land use. Kenya is visited by up to 300,000 adult tourists each year, bringing in some $200 million – there is no doubt that elephants are one of the main attractions. Thus, elephants play a central role in the economy as well as the ecology of the countries they inhabit. They are the "flagship" of the wildlife conservation movement. If we cannot save the elephants, what hope is there for the lesser creatures whose fate rests in our hands.

"I first saw elephants in their natural habitat when my father took me to Africa in 1946. They were altogether different from their sad relatives confined to circuses

and zoos. So abundant were the herds, I could hardly have imagined that one day I would be involved in international efforts to save them from extinction."
Prince Sadruddin Aga Khan
President, The Bellerive Foundation

Since its launch in May 1989, ELEFRIENDS has rapidly grown into a major conservation movement, supported by more than one million people worldwide, including many internationally known celebrities.

The ELEFRIENDS campaign has two objectives – to support effective anti-poaching in the field and to tackle the consumer markets for ivory around the world.

Elephant numbers have fallen by over fifty per cent in the last ten years. As long as there are still people wanting to buy and trade ivory – even illegally – there will still be poachers willing to devastate the remaining herds.

It is up to us to persuade consumers all around the world that ivory, far from being desirable, is the product of a sickening, cruel mass slaughter.

Through the effort of elefriendly volunteers, ELEFRIENDS is continually raising funds to support the following: anti-poaching initiatives in a number of African countries including Tanzania, Nigeria, Ghana and Chad; the production of targeted information packs for distribution in countries where ivory is still sold and continued monitoring of the ivory trade. Please help us.

For more information about ELEFRIENDS, please contact:

The Overlook Press

RR 1 Box 496

Woodstock, New York 12498

The author and publishers wish to thank all of those who gave quotes for the book. Some appeared in earlier publications as listed below, but most were given to ELEFRIENDS at the time of its launch in 1989 or during the preparation of this book. Page 13 Heathcote Williams, *Sacred Elephant*, Cape 1989; page 25 Charles F Holder, *The Ivory King*, Scribners 1866; page 27 Cynthia Moss, *Elephant Memories*, Elm Tree Books 1988; page 28 Dr Iain Douglas-Hamilton, *Among The Elephants*, Collins 1975; page 33 Dr Joyce Poole, *Animal Kingdom*; page 38 Dr S Keith Eltringham, *Elephants*, Blandford 1982; page 45 Captain Richard Meinertzhagen, *Kenyan Diary*, 1903.

The author and publishers wish to thank the following for permission to use copyright material:
HEATHER ANGEL pp 16-17; **ARDEA LONDON** pp 10 *top* Masahiro Iijima, 12 *top* P Morris, 39 *top left* John Wightman, 39 *bottom right* Jim and Julie Bruton and 46-47 Julie Bartlett; **DAVID BACK/ICCE** pp 22-23; **JEN AND DES BARTLETT/SURVIVAL ANGLIA** p 35 *bottom*; **MARK BOULTON/ICCE** pp 26-27 *main spread*; **PHILIP CAYFORD** title page, pp 5 and 44-45 *main spread*; **BRUCE COLEMAN LIMITED** pp 14 *both*, 15 *bottom*, 20-21, 29, 30 and 31 *top*; **ENVIRONMENTAL INVESTIGATION AGENCY** pp 4 *both* and 45 *both*; **FRANK LANE PICTURE AGENCY LTD** pp 37 *top* and 39 *bottom left*; **HUGO VAN LAWICK/NATURE PHOTOGRAPHERS LTD** pp 8-9, 31 *bottom*, 34, 35 *top*, 37 *bottom* and 39 *top right*; **P C LEE** p 32; **MIKE MOCKLER/SWIFT PICTURE LIBRARY** p 10 *bottom*; **OXFORD SCIENTIFIC FILMS** pp 15 *top* G I Bernard and 48 Richard Packwood; **RICHARD PACKWOOD** pp 11 *bottom*, 33 and 38; **DIETER PLAGE/SURVIVAL ANGLIA** p 40; **JONATHAN SCOTT/ PLANET EARTH PICTURES** pp 7 *bottom* and 41.

The photographs on pages 6, 11 *top*, 12 *bottom*, 13, 18 *both*, 19, 24 *both*, 25, 27 *bottom*, 28, 36 *all* and 42-43 are courtesy of **IAN REDMOND**. The photograph on page 7 *top* is courtesy of **WILL TRAVERS**.

Front cover: **OXFORD SCIENTIFIC FILMS** Richard Packwood; Back cover: **BRUCE COLEMAN LIMITED, NATURE PHOTOGRAPHERS, OXFORD SCIENTIFIC FILMS** Richard Packwood; Endpapers: **VISIONS PHOTO INC.**